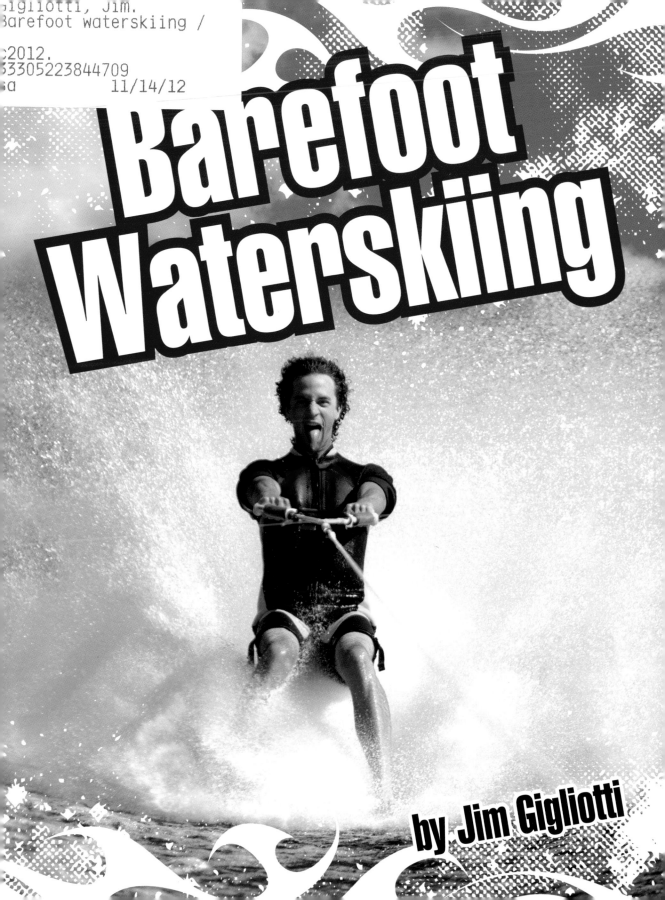

Barefoot Waterskiing

by Jim Gigliotti

Published by The Child's World®
1980 Lookout Drive
Mankato, MN 56003-1705
800-599-READ
www.childsworld.com

The Child's World®: Mary Berendes, Publishing Director
Shoreline Publishing Group, LLC: James Buckley Jr.,
   Production Director
The Design Lab: Design and production

ISBN: 978-1-60973-177-9
LCCN: 2011928870

Photo credits: Cover: Photos.com.
Interior: AP/Wide World: 24; Corbis: 8, 11;
dreamstime.com: Monkey Business Images 15,
Maurice Hill 20; Lauren Lane Lindeman: 12, 19, 23, 27;
USA Water Ski: 4, 28.

Printed in the United States of America
Mankato, Minnesota
July, 2011
PA02094

Table of Contents

Elaine Heller shows off her record-setting water-ski jumping form.

CHAPTER ONE

Extreme Waterskiing

Elaine Heller skis toward the small, blue ramp poking out of the water. She holds onto the handle of a long towrope. A motorboat pulls her along the water at almost 45 miles per hour (72 kph). Elaine is all focus and determination at the 2010 World Championships in Brandenburg, Germany. The boat zooms past the ramp. Elaine rides up the ramp and soars through the air. She splashes back down: 69 feet (21 meters). The crowd roars. Her jump is a new world record!

Oh, by the way, did we mention that Elaine is doing this *barefoot*?

That's right. Elaine is part of a group of water-skiers that has taken their sport to an extreme level: They don't use skis! These athletes like the challenge of skiing without skis.

When it's done right, the water feels as smooth as glass. When it's not done right, it can be a pretty rough ride. And losing your balance can mean a hard fall—face first. Ouch!

The wind in his face . . . and nothing on his feet: This barefoot waterskier shows how much fun this sport can be.

A color postcard pictures Dick Pope Jr. showing off this new water sport.

Barefoot waterskiing is one of the few extreme sports that can spot its exact beginning. According to the Water Ski Hall of Fame, the sport began in 1947. That year in Winter Haven, Florida, a 17-year-old named A.G. Hancock first tried to waterski without skis. That same year, champion waterskier Dick Pope Jr. was the first man to be photographed skiing barefoot on the water.

Word of barefoot waterskiing spread to Australia. The folks "Down Under" quickly took to the sport. Australia produced the first world champions: Brett Wing on the men's side, and Colleen Wilkinson on the women's side.

In 1950, the first barefoot waterskiing competition was held. The only event was to see who could stay up on the water the longest! Soon, barefoot water-skiers (or "barefooters," for short) began doing tricks.

Americans Don Thompson and Randy Rabe were among the first barefoot waterskiing stars. They are often credited with inventing the sport's **standard tricks** in the 1960s.

The most famous American barefoot waterskier got his start in the 1950s and 1960s. "Banana" George Blair got lots of attention for his amazing tricks. He was still waterskiing barefoot when he was in his nineties! Why "Banana"? He loved to perform wearing a bright yellow wetsuit.

Today, barefoot waterskiing events are held around the world. In the United States, the **sanctioning body** for the sport is the American Barefoot Waterski Club (ABC). The ABC holds tournaments throughout the summer in Kansas, Minnesota, Texas, Wisconsin, and other places.

So, are you ready to go barefooting? Let's go—but don't forget to leave your skis behind!

Using a special mouthpiece, "Banana" George
can water-ski without using skis . . . or hands!

This young skier has learned her lessons well.

CHAPTER TWO

Learning to Go Barefoot

Barefoot waterskiers minimize **friction** to glide over the water. They do that with a combination of balance and body position. It's pretty tricky, especially at first. It takes a good teacher to show a beginner how to get it right.

If you think you want to learn to water-ski barefoot, there's one key step. Before you go near the water, make sure you can be safe *in* the water. Because if you water-ski, you're going to get wet!

First, you've got to be a great swimmer. Take swimming lessons from a qualified instructor. Then, find a **professional** instructor for barefoot skiing lessons. Have a parent help you find a teacher or club that can help you learn. There's all kinds of information available on the Internet now.

Barefooters need a boat that will tow them fast enough. It takes more speed to tow a barefoot skier than a regular waterskier. There are even special boats for barefooters. Those boats make smaller **wakes**.

The right gear is important, too. Barefooters need a life jacket and padded shorts—water can pack a punch when you smack into it! Bulky life jackets can make doing tricks a bit difficult. So experienced barefooters sometimes wear a wetsuit with a life vest built in. Tricks are strictly for **veteran** barefooters, though. Beginners have to master the basics first!

This skier's shirt has a life vest sewn into it.

Young skiers can learn by riding on a boom like this one.

Skiers learning to go barefoot sometimes use a boom instead of a cable or rope. The boom is a long pole attached to the side of the boat. Using the boom has some advantages for a beginner. The skier is a lot closer to the instructor. It's easier to hear advice being shouted over the rush of water and the sound of the boat's engine. It's also easier to get going again after a fall. For that reason, even experienced barefooters sometimes use a boom. It helps them work on new tricks or techniques.

Beginners might even consider using shoe skis, too. They fit snugly over the feet. They feel almost like barefooting, but help reduce friction. Some traditional barefoot waterskiers will argue that it's not really barefooting if you have shoe skis on! Shoe skis, though, help beginners learn. The boat doesn't have to go as fast to keep the skier upright. And it's easier to learn different **maneuvers** first with the shoe skis. Then they can come off, and it's nothing but bare feet!

This skier is wearing shoe skis while he practices this difficult move.

Here's a great demonstration of the front-to-back move.

The World Barefoot Council's rule book details a whole . . . well, boatload of barefoot waterskiing tricks. Here are a few.

- **Front-to-Back:** In regular barefoot skier position (BSP), the skier does a 180-degree turn to backward BSP. A Back-to-Front, of course, is just the opposite.

- **Wake Hop:** From outside the wake on one side, the barefooter jumps over the wake and lands on its other side.

- **The Side Slide:** The skier rotates both feet 90 degrees to the line of the boat's path.

- **Tumbleturn:** From a standing position, the barefooter goes down on his or her bottom. He or she spins around (that's where those padded shorts help!) while maintaining hold of the handle, then stands back up.

CHAPTER THREE

Barefoot's Best

The best barefooters in the world go toe-to-toe at major international events. Most barefoot contests have three parts: slalom, tricks, and jumping. The rules are set by the World Barefoot Council.

In the slalom, skiers cross back and forth over their boat's wake. They have 15 seconds to completely cross over. They have two passes (or tries), one forward and one backward.

In the tricks portion, skiers do as many tricks as they can in two 15-second passes. They are awarded points for each trick. They can do several easy tricks, or go for harder ones that are worth more points if done right.

A tumbleturn like this one could score big points during the tricks event.

It's a bird, it's a plane . . . it's a barefoot waterski jumper!

In jumping, it's all about distance. Barefooters found they go farther if they jump **inverted** (which means upside-down!). Great Britain's David Small set a world record when he jumped 98 feet (29.9 meters) in 2010. Elaine Heller, who set the women's record that year, was the first female to jump inverted.

Inverted jumpers go heels over head when they jump. After takeoff they bring their feet up high in the air. It looks almost as if they are ready to dive into the water. Then they yank back on the rope handle. That brings them back to an upright position for landing. It's a dangerous move—and absolutely not for beginners. Even for the most experienced jumpers wear helmets.

World Barefoot Championships have been held every two years since 1978. At first, the Australians dominated the team event. But since the United States won its first title in 1986, Americans have been unbeatable—13 wins in a row!

Elaine Heller was the women's overall champion in Germany in 2010. The American star is ranked No. 2 in the world entering 2011. Australia's Ashleigh Stebbings is No. 1. On the men's side, Great Britain's David Small is No. 1. He won his third individual world championship in 2010.

David Small shows off the form that has made him a three-time world champ.

Side-by-side, these Figure 8 racers
see who can hold on for the longest time.

In the United States, the ABC runs a new type of race. It's an **endurance** event called Figure 8. In the Figure 8, two barefooters are towed by the same boat. Each barefooter stays on one side of the wake while the boat makes figure 8 patterns on the water. Whichever skier stays up the longest wins.

The Figure 8 is a test of endurance and concentration. Skiers have to battle their opponent and their own fatigue. They also deal with winds and choppy water, too. The Figure 8 is taking the extreme sport of barefoot waterskiing to another extreme!

Glossary

endurance—being able to do one thing steadily for a long period of time

friction—when two objects or surfaces rub against each other (in this case, feet and water) and reduce motion

inverted—turned upside down

maneuvers—movements or tactics

professional—someone who is paid to do a job that requires special training or education

sanctioning body—an organization that makes and enforces the rules of a sport

standard—typical

veteran—a person who has been involved with a sport for several years or more

wakes—trails left in the water by a boat

BOOKS

Water Sports (Extreme Sports)
By Bob Woods. Milwaukee, WI: Gareth Stevens Publishing, 2003.
This book offers a look at some of the other extreme ways to have fun on the water.

WEB SITES

For links to learn more about extreme sports: **childsworld.com/links**

Note to Parents, Teachers, and Librarians: We routinely verify our Web links to make sure they are safe and active sites. So encourage your readers to check them out!

Index

About the Author

Jim Gigliotti is a former editor at the National Football League. He has written more than 50 books about sports for youngsters and adults.